HER BELOVED
DRAGON MATE

A CRESCENT LAKE SHIFTERS STORY

ARIZONA TAPE

BLURB

Only the full moon can reveal the truth about her mate.

Dragon shifter, Ruby, can't wait to spend the rest of her life with Hannah but without knowing if they're fated, she's not sure if she's ready to commit.

Everything about Drakefield is elusive and new to Hannah, but she's ready to embrace this hidden world and its unusual customs. Or so she thinks...

Will Hannah and Ruby discover they're meant for each other or will the truth break their hearts?

-

Her Beloved Dragon Mate is a fated mates paranormal romance featuring a dragon shifter and her mate. It includes a standalone f/f romance and a dash of steamy goodness. It is part of the Crescent Lake Shifters series.

ONE

RUBY

THE REFLECTION of the full moon rippled like liquid silver in the crescent lake underneath but the breathtaking view was lost on Ruby and most of the inhabitants of Crescent Valley. It was the group of giggling, chattering humans on the other side of the clearing that held her attention and focus.

Despite the chill in the air and the lack of clothes, Ruby felt perfectly comfortable. Most shifters hadn't bothered covering up and were waiting fully nude for the signal. The other side was a different story, most humans were covered up in some way.

Ruby's eye landed on a beautiful blonde in a

bikini dotted with roses, her breath hitching. She couldn't wait until they met in the water.

"Rubes. Is that you?" a familiar voice said from her left.

She turned, smiling at the sight of the wolf shifter pushing through the sea of bodies to her side. "Hey, Cate. Fancy seeing you here. Haven't seen you since sixth grade."

The shorter, stockier woman chuckled. "I know. Graduation, hehe. Which one's yours?"

With a big grin, Ruby pointed at the blonde on the other side. "Hannah, the one in pink."

"Nice," her friend remarked appreciatively. "Mine is Trevor, the commando one next to the girl in the blue swimming suit."

"I like his confidence," Ruby remarked, happy to make distracting small talk so she wasn't counting down the seconds until the long-awaited and dreaded jump. After tonight, everything could be different.

Not wanting to fall into the pit of worries, she turned her attention to her school friend. "How long have you two been together?"

"A year. You?"

"Almost two."

"And you're only now taking the plunge?" Cate inquired.

Ruby nodded. "We wanted to be sure. Oh, shh-shh, the torches are being lit."

The group of shifters around her fell silent and the attention shifted upward to the small congress of village leaders. Ruby recognised the Elder Lorna from Drakefield but she wasn't familiar with the other representatives from the surrounding shifter towns.

"Welcome to the night of the full moon where all your dreams or nightmares can come true," Lorna announced, her voice effortlessly carrying over the crowd. "The water will reveal the truth you seek, but only to those who are brave enough to risk it all."

"Why does everything have to be spoken in riddles?" Cate whispered softly. "Truth we seek, blah blah blah. Can't she hurry up with her damn speech? I want to jump in so I can get my mating mark."

Ruby wisely didn't reply, not wanting to start a fight by calling out the wolf shifter on her disrespect. She held the Moon Goddess and the rituals under great regard and was happy to be a part of the ancient tradition. Speeches and all.

"The mark will reveal the Moon Goddesses' will and with it, your own," Elder Lorna added with her strong voice. She gestured to the open water of the crescent lake. "As always, the hosts will enter first."

"May the moon bless you," Ruby wished to her

classmate. She raced to the water in synch with the rest of her side. A few used the opportunity to shift and a blur of dark fur and claws flashed by her left while a scaly wing barely missed her on the right. She almost regretted not shifting herself but she didn't want to meet Hannah that way.

The mayhem and chaos didn't stop when she hit the water. The sudden cold hitched her breath and she gasped as she swam deeper into the silver lake. Someone accidentally kicked her in the side and she mowed her arms in wild desperation, trying to get away from the mass and get some space for herself. Not too deep, not too shallow, somewhere perfect where Hannah would be able to find her easily.

She waited with bated breath and the wave of a torch brought the next signal. The human side charged for the water with as much enthusiasm and cheering, disturbing the lake once more.

Ruby's heart pounded as she lost track of Hannah in the rowdy crowd of bodies. She scanned the rippling water for her girlfriend, searching for the rose bikini or her blonde head. An impossible task and even though she knew that was the purpose of the ritual, she loathed it at the moment.

Unable to do anything but wait, she floated in the water with just the hope and belief in her heart that fate would guide Hannah to her.

Someone swam to her and she perked up but her hope was quickly dashed when she realised it was an unknown man. She continued searching the crowd of bopping heads, waiting for the sign of the universe that she and Hannah were meant to be. Despite the full moon and her heightened eyesight, it was nearly impossible to distinguish the people in the water from the woman she knew so well.

Painstaking minutes passed in which shifters all around her united with the people they brought but Ruby was still alone. Part of her worried that Hannah hadn't made the jump in the first place and she was waiting in vain. Or worse, that another shifter had caught her attention and she'd changed her mind.

With a grimace, she shook the doubts away. Hannah wouldn't do that to her. She would find her and they'd wake up with matching marks in the morning, she just knew it.

A splash drew her attention and relief crashed over her as she spotted the familiar blonde swimming leisurely towards her.

"You made it," Ruby exclaimed, welcoming her desperately with open arms.

Hannah spluttered a chuckle as she latched on. "Of course. I love you, did you not think I'd find you?"

"I love you too. Let's get out of here." She said, nudging towards the shore.

"Do we not need to stay longer?" Hannah inquired, struggling to stay afloat.

"No, we've found each other so the ritual is complete. Let's talk more when we're not drowning," she joked.

Back on land, they grabbed a set of pre-prepared towels and wrapped themselves up tight. With one arm around Hannah's back, Ruby guided her up the path to the main building that doubled as a hotel on this particular night.

"A room for two," Ruby ordered at the front desk, her arm still tightly around Hannah. In her heart of hearts, she'd never doubted that the two of them would emerge together but she wouldn't feel secure until the morning revealed whether they'd been blessed with matching marks or not.

TWO

HANNAH

NOT FOR THE FIRST TIME, the warmth of the tangled bedsheets and wall of pillows made Hannah feel like she woke up in a large nest of sorts. She snuggled into the comforting smell of pinewood and ash until she remembered the significance of the morning.

Her eyes flew open and she shook the woman next to her.

Ruby jolted up from the movement, her dark hair a nest of its own. Confused, she scratched the side of her face. "Did I wake you?"

The first chuckle of the day escaped Hannah's lips. "No, I woke you. You're nesting again."

"I am?" the other woman yawned as she unfurled, leaving a scaly imprint in the sheets underneath her. "Sorry, I didn't notice."

"It's okay, I'm mostly used to it by now. It's morning," she announced with bated breath.

Ruby's eyes widened but she didn't move a muscle. "Have you checked yet?"

"I haven't, I'm too nervous."

"We'll do it together. Ready?"

Hannah gathered a tense breath before nodding and pushing the blankets away. She released an immediate sigh at the unfamiliar mark on her right wrist, instantly feeling a bit better. "I've got one," she announced, turning the tattoo-like mark towards her girlfriend. "You?"

Next to her, Ruby tilted her hips. "Here, is it the same?"

Despite her jitters, Hannah brought her wrist to the other woman's lower body and held it there to compare the intricate marks. Thin lines swirled and curled in perfect opposites of each other and glowed faintly red when joined together.

The two women breathed a sigh of relief.

"We're marked," Ruby said in a quiet voice.

"We're marked?" Hannah gasped as Ruby catapulted herself on her, attacking her with a barrage of affectionate kisses.

"We're marked! Now I can do this."

Hannah watched with curiosity as the dark-haired woman rummaged through her clothes on the floor and presented her with a small velvet box. She gasped at the prospect, her chest filling with flutters. "Are you serious?"

"Drakely serious. Hannah Montgomery, will you make me the happiest dragon in the world and marry me?"

She smothered a whimper and nodded enthusiastically. "Yes, I will. Yes!"

Her hand trembled as she held it out for Ruby to slide the engagement ring on her finger. The warm gold complimented her skin nicely and the brilliant red stone in the middle matched the fire in Ruby's eyes.

"I think this warrants a celebration," Hannah murmured, snaking her arm around the dark-haired woman and pulling her on top of her.

"I agree," the other woman returned suggestively.

A warm glow engulfed Hannah as she held her fiancée in her arms. The biggest smile split her face at the new term. Fiancée. It would take her a while to get used to it but she couldn't be happier about it

From what she'd heard whispered around in Crescent Valley and the Silver City, the full moon ritual could make or break a relationship. While the marking wasn't binding and could be ignored, plenty of the shifters regarded it as a sign of fate. Mating someone without the blessing's mark was highly discouraged.

Hannah wasn't sure if Ruby believed in the sanctity of the mark and whether returning without one would've been the end of the relationship, but she was also desperately glad she didn't have to find out.

A familiar tune played from the phone on the bed stand on Ruby's side, vibrating the whole side table. Hannah laughed at the interruption and the frustrated scowl on Ruby's face as she was forced to answer. She watched her fiancée pace up and down the room, admiring the way the light caught on her body and created smooth shadows and inviting curves. She hoped the call wasn't important but the growing worry on Ruby's beautiful face was telling a different story.

"Everything okay?" Hannah asked once the phone call was over.

Ruby groaned, a different kind than before, and pinched the bridge of her nose. "Yeah, it's fine, my dad's car broke down so I need to take my little brother to school. Why is he calling me? He knows it's the morning after the full moon."

"Can't he walk to work? Or better yet, fly?"

Hannah attempted, slowly trailing a hand up her hip in the hope to entice her fiancée back to the bed.

"I wish."

She could tell from Ruby's tone that her mind was made up and while she usually admired and adored her fiancée's dedication to her family, it sucked when it spoiled the mood. Nonetheless, Hannah knew it was for the best and she didn't want to be late for her own job either.

"It's okay, we knew this would happen with the full moon being in the middle of the work week. I'm still glad we went instead of waiting," she concluded, hopping off the bed and making her way over to the dark-headed woman. She reached out to gingerly twist Ruby's cheek and captured her in a promising kiss. "But we're going to have some fun later."

Ruby's lips tweaked up in a smirk. "You bet, mate-to-be."

The remark had Hannah laughing on her way to the bathroom. "Right back at you, bride-to-be."

"I love you!" she called after her. "We'll celebrate properly. Tonight? I have to swing by my flat for clean clothes but I can meet you after."

"I'm working late tonight so tomorrow? Dinner at our usual restaurant?" Hannah proposed, lingering on the threshold.

When she got confirmation, she disappeared into

the bathroom, not able to stop grinning. Standing in front of the mirror, she had to admit she hadn't looked this happy in a long time. Something about Ruby just made her feel more loved and relaxed than any other point in her life and she wanted to share the good news with her family, even if she wasn't entirely sure what the Crescent Moon Ceremony would entail or what she could and couldn't share about the dubious nature of Drakefield.

THREE

RUBY

RUBY STEPPED INTO THE RESTAURANT, the savoury smell of whatever was cooking greeting her at the door. As usual, she'd arrived early and before Hannah but she didn't mind. She'd order herself a drink and happily wait for her mate to celebrate the marking and engagement.

With a smile, she briefly touched her hip. Even through her clothes, she could feel the new mark and the connection to its counterpart. It was like she carried a little part of Hannah with her, even more so than before.

"We have a reservation," she told the server at the door. "Callahan, table for two, but I'm a bit early."

The man in the black waistcoat nodded and gestured inside. "Welcome. Would you like to wait at the bar or your table?"

"I'll wait at the bar," Ruby decided when she spotted her best friend tending it. She crossed the restaurant, avoiding passing directly next to occupied tables as not to interrupt.

There were a few people at the bar and she picked a seat near the curved end so she could keep the door in view. She drummed her fingers on the bar, instantly regretting it when they came into contact with the sticky surface. "Barkeep, this needs cleaning."

"You little—" Kendra turned with a bemused scowl, running a hand through her slick short hair.

Ruby narrowly caught the damp cloth the woman tossed her way and wiped the bar with mocking attitude. "What kind of service is this?"

"Better than you deserve. Rum?"

"No, I'm waiting for Hannah. I'll have some spring water with lime. Actually, make that sparkling. We're celebrating."

"Sparkling water? You're pulling out all the stops." Kendra returned with a tall glass and the requested lime. "On the house. How did things go at the lake yesterday? Good, I presume, since you're here celebrating instead of drowning your sorrows."

"Very good, indeed." Ruby lifted her shirt to reveal part of the new mark on her hip. "I proposed."

"That's wonderful! I'm so excited for you." Her childhood friend hummed in approving agreement. "I like Hannah, she's a good egg."

"She is. She's the one."

"I'm really pleased for you."

"Thanks." Ruby took a sip from her sparkling water. "So what's up with you? I haven't seen you in a while."

"That's because you're practically living at Hannah's."

"You don't mind, do you?"

"No, I like having the place to myself," Kendra replied, waggling her eyebrows. "Don't have to be quiet."

"You weren't quiet when I was there either," Ruby pointed out, smiling in bemusement. "How's the firm?"

"No idea."

She raised an eyebrow. "You're really not keeping in touch with your dad?"

"Nope. He can shove his nepotism and his law firm where the sun doesn't shine. I'm not talking to him until the apologises."

"I'm sorry things are strained at the moment. I hope you can work things out," Ruby said earnestly, remembering how close Kendra used to be to with her father.

The other woman shrugged. "It's fine. I'm enjoying working here, mostly because it infuriates him, and I'll figure something out. I'm young, I've got my whole future ahead of me."

"That's the spirit. Well, if I can do something, just let me know." Ruby finished her water and turned when she heard the little bell by the door, glad to see Hannah. "That's my date."

"Say hi to Hannah for me. I presume you're not going to sleep at the flat tonight then?" Kendra winked.

"I hope not."

"Great because I'm pretty sure I'll have company." Kendra's gaze landed on the blonde at the end of the bar.

"You're such a flirt. Be safe and at least make her breakfast." She retreated with a wave, her thoughts no longer with best friend and instead, focused on the beautiful woman entering the restaurant.

She greeted her with a quick but intimate kiss, her mood instantly lifting. "Hello, beautiful."

Hannah's face lit up. "Hi. Have you been waiting long?"

"A little bit, but I caught up with Kendra," Ruby answered, gesturing in the direction of the bar where the short-haired blonde was flirting shamelessly. She smiled at her best friend's behaviour and while she thought fondly back to the time they picked up women together, she couldn't say she missed it. Not when she had Hannah.

"Shall we sit?" she proposed, gesturing to one of the free tables.

They ordered food and chatted about nothing in particular until it arrived.

"I've been thinking about how to tell my sister about our engagement," Hannah confessed as she took a bite of her lasagne. "Wow, this is delicious. Do you want to try it?"

Ruby nodded, offering her a bite from her cutlet in exchange. She hummed in appreciation, but was still preferred her choice. With a smile, she returned to the topic at hand. "You can tell them whichever way you like."

"Miranda can just be a bit… much." She hesitated. "You know I'm looking forward to our union, right? But this whole mating ceremony is just a bit foreign to me. You've said there might be other people?"

"Yes, but they'll go through the ceremony before or after us. And only dragons, the other shifters have their own spots by the lake," Ruby explained, reaching across the table. "This is our wedding and we can do it whichever way we like."

"It just has to be by the Crescent Lake."

"If we want to be mated, yes, and it has to be during a waxing moon. Otherwise the fated bond won't take hold." Ruby hesitated. "We don't have to if you don't want. We can just get human married."

Hannah chuckled lightly. "We can't."

"Why not?"

"Because you just called it human married. I want us to be bound in the eyes of your society too."

Touched by the explanation, Ruby brought Hannah's hand up and pressed a kiss on the slender knuckles. "You're sweet. I'm sorry I called it human married, to me it's just... that. A piece of paper, a contract. But being mated, bonded together by the moon, it's deeper than that. It's our soul."

"That's what being married is too."

"You say that now. Wait until the bond is sealed and you'll know what I'm talking about," she promised, releasing her hand so they could continue to eat.

After the plates were cleared and more small talk was made, Hannah returned to the original topic. "And you're sure my friends and family are allowed at the mating ceremony?" Hannah checked, despite having already asked multiple times.

"Of course, it's your wedding. Dessert?" Ruby proposed, passing the menu across the table.

"Only if there's ice cream. But what if they find out about you? About this town?"

"They won't," Ruby assured her. "There's vanilla, tropical, and cherry."

"But what if they do?"

"Then we'll deal with it. It's not the end of the world if they discover I'm a dragon," Ruby said, finally realising this warranted more than a passing reassurance. She smiled warmly at the other woman, overcome with affection. "You can just tell them if you want. They're your family so they'll be my family. It's only a secret from the world, not from those close to us. Most people here in the Silver City are humans who know about our existence. Some outside too, although they might choose to believe it's all folklore and myths."

Relief flitted through her when Hannah visibly relaxed. "I'm not sure I want to tell my sister but it makes me feel better that I can." She picked up the dessert menu. "I want tropical. I assume you'll have cherry?"

"You know me so well."

"That's because you love red food."

"It comes with the territory of being a ruby dragon."

That made Hannah chuckle. "Your parents really weren't very original in picking your name."

"Nope, they were not. And there were three more Rubies in my year too. So lame."

"Well, I only have eyes for one," Hannah flirted, her lips curling up into something of a smirk.

The subtle change of her tone didn't go unnoticed by Ruby and she felt a little thrill of excitement running down her back. The pressure felt achingly familiar and the sudden urge to shift caught her off guard. It swirled in her chest, pushing outwards against her ribcage in an attempt to break free.

"Are you okay?" Hannah asked, concern colouring her face.

"Hmm-hmm, give me a moment." Ruby strained against the growing need, puffing and panting to gain control of her breathing.

She focused on Hannah's worried eyes, using the clear blues to centre herself. She couldn't lose control in the middle of their favourite restaurant. Besides scaring the citizens of the Silver City, she'd get a huge fine and she'd also terrify Hannah. That was the last thing she wanted.

The tingling in her back receded and she could breathe again without her chest feeling like it was going to explode. She sighed in relief, glad she was in control once more. She hadn't felt like that since puberty when her dragon was a lot more volatile and hadn't fully merged with her yet. There hadn't been any resistance or rebellion since she came of age so why was the dragon stirring now?

She looked at Hannah, her gaze flicking to the mark on her wrist. Was this a consequence of the moon ceremony or was something else going on?

FOUR

Hannah

Waiting under the warm sun, Hannah smiled as her sister Miranda bounced out of the arriving train and practically bulldozed through the crowd to give her a hug.

"It's too hot for that," Hannah said, jokingly pushing her older sister away.

"Then you shouldn't live so far away," Miranda scolded, swatting her shoulder. "Show me the ring!"

Bemused and only in mock-reluctance, Hannah held out her hand. The ruby stone caught in the sunlight and shimmered in the same way as the woman who gave it to her. An unconventional choice of a ring for a regular engagement, but not for a dragon. Not that she was going to reveal that little tidbit to her older sister.

"No diamond?" Miranda gawked at the jewel, studying it with critical eyes.

Hannah chuckled as she pulled her hand back, not at all surprised at her sister's comment. "You're too obsessed with tradition. Ruby is… different, the whole Callahan clan is. You'll understand when you meet her."

The two women chattered on their way to the spot she chose for lunch, the topic ranging from the proposal, to the occupants of the street they grew up on, and the irritating people Miranda met on the train.

They arrived at the bistro and a smell of freshly baked bread and savoury meat greeted them at the door. Hannah chose a table in the corner and a woman with bushy eyebrows brought them water and menus. After living in the Silver City for a few year, Hannah had gotten pretty good at distinguishing the paranormal and she suspected the woman serving them a wolf shifter from a nearby town. There was just something about the vibe, the way the air changed around them. She watched her sister closely but Miranda seemed none the wiser about who or what was serving them.

She smiled, reminiscing back to the days she herself had been oblivious to the mysteries of the world.

"You haven't told me when the wedding is," Miranda said as she ordered a greasy burger.

"Do you want to share a bottle of wine?" Hannah said, a sly attempt to divert the conversation.

"Naturally and don't change the subject." The other woman sat up, suddenly looking worried. She waited until the server had left with their orders before speaking again. "Han? Is there something the matter?"

"No, nothing as such. The wedding is this weekend so I was thinking this could be kind of like my hen party?" Hannah wasn't sure why she phrased it as a question, she was the one who picked this waxing moon instead of waiting for a later date. "And I was hoping you'd be my maid of honour."

"What? Of course, I'll be your maid of honour, but next week? Why the rush? If Ruby is pressuring you, you can tell me."

Hannah paused, not sure how to explain it without exposing Ruby's true nature and how this wedding wasn't just a wedding. Her sister wouldn't understand and to a degree, even she couldn't fully comprehend the magnitude of it.

Deciding to keep the reveal for another time, she

smiled. "Nobody is pressuring me, I promise. Ruby is amazing and so patient. We picked the date together and you know I don't like planning far ahead. I like doing things in the now."

"Which is super weird considering your job is to plan things," Miranda pointed out.

Hannah could tell that her sister wasn't fully convinced yet but she knew that if she saw her and Ruby together, she'd be able to see the undeniable bond. She sipped from her refreshing lemon water and smiled. "I want to get married this weekend. Ruby is amazing, you'll love her." She paused, choking up. "Dad would've loved her too."

A faraway look replaced Miranda's smile as she averted her gaze. "I'm sorry he can't be at the wedding."

"It's okay, I've got you and I'll have my friends." Hannah reached out to her sister, clasping her hand tightly. "And I know he'll be with me in spirit. He always is."

The wolf shifter returning with drinks broke the emotional hold over the two women and the brief interruption drove the grief back into its cage. Hannah forced herself to smile, not because she had to keep up pretences, but because she wanted to choose a life of happiness and joy.

It seemed like her sister picked up on her wishes

and conjured a smile in return. "So who else is coming to this impromptu hen party? Tess, I presume. And Christian."

"Tess couldn't get the weekend off, too short notice."

Miranda hummed. "Did you invite Jodi?"

"Of course, she's my friend."

"She's also your ex," the other woman pointed out.

"I'm an adult, I can be friends with my ex," Hannah defended herself. "Besides, it was a long time ago."

She could tell her sister wasn't convinced by this either but her phone vibrated on the table, giving her an excuse to drop the subject. Her cheeks flushed slightly when she noticed the message was from Jodi but she quickly reminded herself that there was no reason to feel guilty.

"Jodi and Christian just arrived at the station, they're coming this way now."

"And was it Jodi or Christian who informed you of that?" Miranda asked with her annoying all-knowing older-sister smirk that Hannah hated.

She drummed her fingers on the table, her nails clicking on the surface. "Jodi, but that doesn't mean anything. Christian's phone is probably dead, or he forgot it, you know what a scatterbrain he is."

"Hmm-hmm. Okay, I believe you," the other woman said in a tune that suggested otherwise.

Not in the mood to be lectured by her older sister, Hannah excused herself to use the facilities and by the time she got back, her friends had arrived. Their presence had driven away the tense atmosphere and Hannah embraced them both with a little extra gratitude.

Christian flashed a lopsided-grin. "Congrats on the engagement."

"Yes and Miranda says it's this Saturday," Jodi added, her clear gaze resting on Hannah. "Why did you say this was just a regular girls weekend? You should've told us and we could've booked all kinds of fun things for us to do. Spas, bars, *strippers*."

With a bemused head shake, Hannah swatted her friend's shoulder. "You know I've never been a stripper girl."

"Boooooring. At least tell me there's going to be an open bar at the wedding."

"I'm not entirely sure, Ruby is doing most of the planning. Weddings are very important in her culture, which is why we're marrying in her hometown."

She felt her sister's scrutinising gaze on her. "Drakefield, right?"

"Drakefield?" Christian echoed. "Isn't that the

town from the urban legend? The one about people being half human-half monster."

Remembering Ruby's words, Hannah chortled. "I haven't seen any monsters yet." A statement that tickled her extra when the wolf-shifter returned to their table to take the newcomers' orders.

"Tequila," Jodi ordered without missing a beat, despite it only being just past noon. "Lots of shots, our girl is getting married."

"We don't serve tequila, this is a bistro," the server replied with one of her bushy eyebrows raised.

"We'll take a bottle of white wine," Hannah quickly said.

Drinks arrived at the table and they chatted and joked about the upcoming nuptials, with Hannah taking the brunt of most jokes. She smiled through them all, enjoying their slight confusion towards her relationship. Ever since she got marked, she could feel a bond to Ruby that hadn't been there before. Not something that constrained her but instead, linked her in a way that gave her security and reassurance but she knew she couldn't put that feeling into words. It didn't worry her, if anything, it bemused her. Like she'd discovered a secret about love that most people weren't privy to. Even if she wanted to share the secret with her friends, it was something that was better discovered first hand.

With a satisfied smile, she raised her glass. "To my wedding."

The other girls cheered and hollered, their excitement outshining the other patrons in the establishment who just wanted a quiet lunch. Hannah shushed the group but their spirits couldn't be contained and their mood was contagious. Soon, they were laughing and giggling as if they were back in school again.

They finished the bottle quickly and moved on to somewhere rowdier to continue the party. In her drunken haze, Hannah missed the curious look from an icy-blonde as they tipsily stumbled past her table, her thoughts only on the upcoming wedding.

FIVE

RUBY

RUBY STOOD in front of the large ornate mirror, fiddling with the button on her burgundy blouse. The traditional colour for a dragon wedding, especially for her clan. She wanted the collar up but the loose material wasn't quite stiff enough.

"Stop, just let it be," Kendra chimed from the seat next to her, a bemused look on her face.

Ruby groaned. "I just want this damned thing to frame my neck. Hannah loves my neck."

"I doubt she'll be looking at *your neck.* You're making me nervous, sit down."

Ignoring her best friend, Ruby attempted to

straighten the fabric once more. She wanted to look perfect so when Hannah laid eyes on her, it would take her breath away. So she would never regret this decision, the decision to become her mate.

"I have a different shirt at home, if you hurry you can get it—"

With a sigh, Kendra rose from her seat, her hand landing on Ruby's shoulder. "Stop, you picked this blouse for a reason. You look wonderful and Hannah isn't going to care if your collar is up or down. Just, breathe, relax, enjoy this last moment of silence before you'll be the centre of attention."

Ruby grumbled but stepped away from the mirror as requested. Even without scrutinising every inch of herself, she could feel the nerves build in her lower stomach, settling like heavy bricks. The mark on her hip pulsed weakly, fainter than the day before and the one before. It would continue to fade until the mating bond was successfully sealed and the lines were redrawn by fate.

She glanced through the window at the opposite building where Hannah was getting ready, finding relief in finding the lights on. That was a good sign, she concluded, especially since she'd seen Hannah's sister enter earlier. Considering there hadn't been bad news, she was reasonably certain that the union was still on.

The pulsing mark certainly suggested so.

She waited for Kendra to return, growing increasingly worried with every passing second. Everything should be ready, why wasn't it?

Her heart jumped when the door opened again and she practically rushed towards Kendra. "So what's the deal? What's taking so long?"

"The officiant spilled wine on her robe but she's ready now."

"And Hannah?"

"Will be there," Kendra said.

"You saw her?" Ruby insisted, her gaze snapping to the other building again.

"No, but I spoke to Jodi, her friend and also her ex? Why is her ex at your wedding?"

Ruby shrugged, barely registering the conversation. She didn't care about the officiant or the ex, she just wanted Hannah to be there. That was all she needed from this night.

With a last look in the mirror and a final adjustment to her collar, she strode out into the night, arriving at the altar first as was custom in the mating union. To give the human the opportunity to change their mind, Ruby realised as she fought her growing worries.

To keep herself from spiralling, she drew her gaze away from the waiting crowd and to the crescent lake at the bottom of the hill where a bear and his mate were entering the water for the rebirth part of the ceremony.

She hoped they'd be gone by the time her and Hannah would descend, not wanting to share the water with another couple. That was supposed to be their moment.

"Why is Hannah not here yet?" Ruby muttered under her breath, not wanting to appear stressed or worried in front of all their friends and family.

The crowd shifted and Ruby's attention travelled to her radiant mate arriving at the end of the aisle escorted by her sister.

Ruby's mouth fell slightly aghast at her approaching mate. Her white dress cascaded down to the ground and her light veil framed her delicate face perfectly. She'd never looked more beautiful and Ruby couldn't believe her luck.

"Hi," she breathed when Hannah reached the altar and placed her hand in hers. Any doubts Ruby had evaporated the moment their fingers touched. She could feel the strength of their bond pulsing through her, shooting straight to the mark on her hip and to her heart. Her dragon stirred again, this time for an entirely different reason.

"Hey," Hannah returned, her eyes shimmering

with adoration and a hint of mischief. "You look hot."

Ruby choked on a snort. "Yes, hot was indeed what I was going for."

The officiant cleared her throat disapprovingly. "Can I begin?"

"Of course," Ruby answered, squeezing Hannah's hand conspiringly. "We're ready."

The torches around her were lit and the harsh smell filled the air with smoke quickly following. It immediately invoked a sense of drama and combined with the waxing moon above their heads, Ruby could feel the magic tingle in the air. She wasn't sure if Hannah could, or the other humans, but it was unmistakable to her. It tickled her nose like spice and reverberated with the call of her dragon inside, awakening something primal and desperate in her.

"I'm here to join Ruby Erin Callahan and Hannah Montgomery in a blessed union of kindred souls in accordance with the law and the rules that bind us. As is traditional, we'll start with the vows. Ruby, you may go first."

Nervously, Ruby cleared her throat in a bid to get her a little extra time. She'd rehearsed the traditional vows so many times, and yet she couldn't remember a single word of it.

"Relax," Hannah whispered, her voice soft and only meant for her. "It's just me."

Ruby released a long breath, her confidence returning to her. "Sorry, I'm just drawing a blank, I have them in my pocket."

"Then why don't I go first?" Hannah volunteered, looking at the officiant. "Is that allowed?"

The Elder hesitated. "It is, but it's unusual for our culture. Are you sure?"

To Ruby's relief, Hannah nodded with her stubborn determination, her eagerness palpable. She could feel the love and respect radiating from her mate-to-be and it erased any lingering doubt about Aisling's accusation.

"My beautiful Ruby," Hannah started, her voice low but clear. "On this day, under the crescent moon, I promise to cherish you, to love you, to sustain you in sickness and in health, in poverty and in wealth, and to be true to you until death do us part."

The sincerity in her words made the mark on Ruby's hip glow hot red and she felt her dragon draw near the surface, still patient... for now.

SIX

HANNAH

HANNAH RELEASED A BREATH OF RELIEF, hoping she hadn't just disrespected Ruby's culture by saying her vows first. From the intense, adoring look in the other woman's eyes, she didn't think so. Ruby looked calm, warm, loving, and much less nervous than before.

She couldn't help but wonder if it was solely about the vows or if there was something else at play. Hannah promised herself she'd inquire about that later but she wasn't going to occupy herself with it now.

Ruby repeated the vows, the slight rasp of her

voice sending tingles down Hannah's spine. The words sounded so much better coming from Ruby's mouth and she felt mesmerised by the promise, almost like it was an enchantment taking hold of her. In a way, she supposed, it was.

The Elder smiled and nodded in acceptance. "Wonderful. I invite you to exchange your rings as a symbol of your commitment and love."

"With this ring I take you as my lawfully wedded wife," Ruby said, her voice thick with emotion.

Hannah's breath hitched as she held out her trembling hand to Ruby, the red stone in her engagement ring shimmering from the surrounding fire. The mark on her wrist grew hotter as Ruby slid the simple golden band on her finger and she could feel the bond between them strengthen.

She felt instantly empowered and she repeated the words effortlessly. Earlier, she worried she'd waver or hesitate at the binding vow but instead, she felt relieved that she'd get to be with Ruby forever. The ring she slid on the other woman's finger was proof of that, a reminder that from that moment on, they were bound together in a way that superseded anything they ever experienced before.

The Elder clapped. "I pronounce you married in the eyes of the law and the laws of the universe. You may kiss each other."

Hannah couldn't lean in quick enough as she captured Ruby in a passionate kiss. She hadn't intended to give their guests a show but caught in the moment, with her heart pounding like a jackhammer and Ruby's supple lips on hers, she didn't care. Her arms wrapped around the other woman out of their own accord as she deepened the kiss, desperate to seal the union.

Lost in the kiss, it took the Elder three coughs to break them apart. "Save some for the honeymoon."

They broke apart, chuckling in each other's embrace. A warm glow settled in Hannah's chest as she regarded the woman in front of her. Her wife.

She smiled as Ruby leaned in for another quick kiss before addressing their friends and family. "As per tradition, Hannah and I will take a private moment to receive the blessing of the Moon Goddess at the lake but there's food and drink waiting for you inside the main building. Please, enjoy. We'll return shortly to celebrate with you and exchange embarrassing stories about each other."

The crowd laughed and as they retreated inside, Hannah followed Ruby down the narrow path to the silver lake.

"What now?" she asked, gesturing to the mirror of water. "I'm not jumping in with my wedding dress, have you seen how much lace there is?"

Ruby chuckled with bemusement. "That's for later, love. This is mostly just an excuse to have a moment to ourselves. How are you feeling? No regrets yet?"

The consideration warmed Hannah and she leaned in, taking advantage of the privacy of the moment. She'd never been so sure of anything and she was desperate to convey her sentiments to her new wife in a way she knew Ruby would understand. Words had always been more her thing but Ruby was a woman of gestures and actions.

They broke apart and Ruby's eyes shimmered with little flames. "So no regrets then."

"Not a single one," Hannah confirmed, glancing over the other woman's shoulder at the quiet lake behind them. It still held mysteries and secrets from her but soon, a new world would unfold itself to her, once she became Ruby's mate.

But first, they were going to celebrate.

Hand in hand, Hannah walked into the main building with Ruby right behind her. Their friends and family cheered upon entry and she noticed Kendra giving Ruby a thumbs-up from by the buffet while her friends were haggling at the bar, even though everything was free.

She smiled at the sight, seeing both their worlds colliding something she'd never imagined possible when she first discovered this hidden world. She'd always assumed everything would be strictly isolated but it seemed most of their secrets relied on the disbelief of humans. She certainly hadn't believe Ruby at first but Hannah was terribly glad she had. Otherwise, she'd have nothing of this.

She reached back to her wife, not wanting to be separated from her for the night. This was their wedding and she fully intended to spend it with Ruby.

"Shall we make our rounds?" Ruby asked, kissing her temple and gesturing to her table seated at the large table in the middle.

Ruby's mother and father hugged Hannah with all the warmth in the world and she melted in their embrace. It felt good to be welcomed with open arms and she felt herself tear up, the emotions of the day catching up with her.

She stepped back, her feelings steadying when Ruby's hand landed on the small of her back. It reassured her, letting her know she wasn't alone. And after today, she'd never be alone again.

SEVEN

RUBY

WHEN THE EXUBERANT night came to an end and the first signs of dawn hinted above the trees, Ruby and Hannah took their leave from the party for the all important next step. Ruby felt giddy and light-headed from all the dancing and laughter, yet there was also a clarity in her mind that she hadn't expected.

She guided Hannah away from the lake, up the darkened path leading towards the elusive Drakefield. It wasn't the first time she'd brought her to her home town but this was different. She could feel the earth calling to her, the magic tingle in the air.

"Tell me about the mating again?" Hannah asked, breaking the silence with a nervous chuckle. "You're actually going to bite me? I guess that's a new way to eat me."

Despite the joke, Ruby heard the concern in her voice and she tensed, worried she hadn't explained things properly before. She paused so she could take Hannah's hands in hers, hoping to reassure her. "Yes, I'm going to bite you but only where you choose and when you say you're ready. It'll sting and you'll bleed a little but it'll heal almost immediately. I've heard it'll also feel good, for both of us, but I only know that from the stories."

Hannah nodded ever so slightly, looking a little less nervous. "So where do you want to do it?"

Ruby considered her options as they set in motion again, still holding hands. "Wherever you want. I've heard the neck is a desirable spot, but the thigh isn't uncommon either."

"I guess when in Rome," Hannah chortled.

A sly smile curled Ruby's lips up and she relaxed, glad they could talk about it. "It doesn't actually have to be during sex, it just has to be before dawn otherwise the moon's power wears off. I believe for some who worship the stars or sun it's a little different but the point is, it's something the couple decides."

"Okay... The neck sounds a little scary, not going to lie."

"And your thighs are ticklish," Ruby added helpfully.

"So are my knees."

Ruby chuckled. "I'm not going to bite your knee."

"You said it could be anywhere." Hannah snickered. "You could bite my cheek."

"I don't want to bite your face," Ruby said, the idea of something going wrong worrying her.

"Not that cheek," Hannah sang.

"Naughty."

They filled the night with laughter and Ruby felt the last of her tension evaporate. She was well aware that everything about her world was different and she'd worried Hannah had only agreed to the mating because it was important to her. The biting, included.

She paused again. "Are you sure you're okay with this?"

Hannah nodded, leaning up to kiss her. "I want to do this with you. I promise. Besides, it doesn't sound too bad, I don't mind the odd graze of your teeth or nip."

"I'm aware," Ruby smirked, gently squeezing the

other woman's hand. Even though she felt more reassured, she didn't feel any less nervous. Maybe even more, knowing the mating was going ahead. This was their last chance to back out. If they went through with it, things would never be the same. The mating bond couldn't be undone, only broken, and it always left a trace. If she bound herself to Hannah, she'd carry her in her heart until the day she died.

Hannah stumbled over a clot of dirt and fell into her, giggling as their bodies met. It broke the lingering tension and a glow filled Ruby as she took the opportunity to pull Hannah in by her hips. Supple and warm, the woman melted into her, her lips parted before hers even reached.

She relished in the languid kiss, the lack of haste a prelude for what was to come.

"I love you," she whispered, looking into Hannah's eyes.

"I love you too."

After a short walk, the forest opened up into one of the sacred clearings with flickering candles and torches the only source of light underneath the crown of trees. Appreciation filled Ruby as she took in the gazebo filled with pillows and blankets. Kendra had outdone herself, she thought, making a note to thank her best friend later for making sure this was all set up for them.

Hannah gasped at the sudden brightness. "Wow, this is beautiful."

"You like it?" Pride pulsed through Ruby as she guided her new wife to the gazebo, gesturing to the heap of plushy cushions. "You should sit."

Hannah's eyes shimmered as she sat down. "Am I finally going to see you?"

She nodded nervously, stepping back so she could make full use of the open space. She was ready to show her true nature, to reveal the last and most intimate thing about herself. Her breath hitched as she fiddled with the buttons of her blouse. Some shifters were a lot more casual about allowing humans to see them in their other form but Ruby had never been like that. This was special to her and she hoped Hannah understood just how much.

Her trembling fingers fought with her shirt as her growing frustration ruined her smooth reveal. This was not how she envisioned it and it was starting to stress her out.

"Want some help?" Hannah offered with a reassuring smile, rising from the pillows.

Ruby thought about protesting and insisting she could do it herself but that defeated the whole point. Instead, she nodded and allowed Hannah to help. She watched as Hannah stepped close, her deft fingers sliding down the trail of buttons, undoing them slowly, teasingly. Every fleeting touch danced on her skin and added to the growing pool of heat in her lower belly.

Her breath hitched as Hannah's hands slid down her sides, opening the shirt and exposing her midriff and stomach to the cool air.

"How's that?" Hannah whispered.

"Perfect. You might want to take a step back now," she suggested. The last thing she wanted was to hurt her beautiful wife and scar her for life.

With Hannah safely back in the gazebo, Ruby let the blouse slide off hers shoulders, embracing the rising morning. She could feel the lingering magic in the air collect around her, reacting to the awakening dragon inside her. The tension around her shoulder blades intensified, the pressure growing with every passing second.

She could feel Hannah's gaze on her and she couldn't remember a time where she'd felt more vulnerable or exposed than this. She guided the magic through her body, allowing it to take over. The pressure against her shoulders roared and her entire body burned from the immense strain. Just when she thought she couldn't take it anymore, her wings pushed out and she exploded in a flurry of scales. Instant relief flooded her as she expanded to her natural size, no longer constricted to by her confines.

The sudden increase made her head spin and it wasn't long until she towered over Hannah and the gazebo. She celebrated in the freedom, raising her large head and stretched her tail as she filled the entire clearing. The sky called to her, tempting her to open her wings and rise, but that wasn't why she shifted.

Ruby denied herself the urge, instead, turning her attention back to Hannah. Her heart pounded in anticipation as she stared at the small figure, silently begging her for approval. Ruby knew how much the other woman loved her but she couldn't deny there'd been a lingering worry that Hannah would change her mind when she was faced with the cold hard reality of what she was. A dragon, or to some, a monster.

Her heart leapt when the other woman approached her.

"Can I touch you?" she asked, her voice clear in the silence of the night.

Ruby nodded her large head, lowering herself gently to the ground. She only relaxed when Hannah's hand brushed down her neck, her fingers dainty on her rough scales. Her touch held no hesitance and Ruby rumbled from the touch, something akin a purr, and surprised herself with the sound. That was new.

"You're beautiful," Hannah whispered, her voice hoarse and low.

To Ruby's surprise, the other woman leaned in and pressed a soft kiss on her large snout, tender and gentle like she wasn't a monstrous beast. It filled her with a newfound appreciation for her wife and gratitude that she accepted her just like that.

She tilted her head, following Hannah as she walked around her, admiring every inch and every scale she had. She could see her confidence growing and the mischief returning in her eyes when she tickled the end of her tail.

With a grin, she flicked it up, making Hannah laugh. The sound evoked another rumble from Ruby's chest and she held still, eagerly letting the other woman explore her body. She recognised the curious touches and discovered they had the same effect on her as when they first slept together. It fanned the growing fire in her belly that was quickly blurring out everything around her except for Hannah.

She rumbled again, enjoying the feel of Hannah's fine fingers and the impossible desire growing in her. She didn't know how long she could take the teasing but she relished in the anticipation. She'd never have another mating and she wanted to savour every single moment of it, engraining and etching it into her memory so she could cherish it forever, just like the beautiful woman she just married.

EIGHT

Hannah

Hannah traced the lines of the ruby scales, the feeling rough and foreign and yet familiar in some way. The more she touched, the more the urge to kiss Ruby grew but she was still in her large dragon form. She wasn't sure whether it was appropriate to ask her to shift back so she kept running her hands along Ruby's body, caressing her with eager hands, hoping to convey her desire.

A shiver ran down her spine as they locked eyes and something in Ruby's changed. Despite never having seen it before, she knew what was about to happen and she stepped back to give her space. Ruby exploded into a whirlwind of glowing scales, a sudden blast of heat taking Hannah off guard. She raised her arm to shield her face, only daring to look when the heat dissipated. The dragon was gone and Ruby was human again, naked and looking rather smug.

Hannah chuckled at the familiar sight and leapt forward, capturing her wife in a kiss laced with desire. The mark on her wrist pulsed and she gasped at the sudden intensity. It hadn't done that before but it sent a little thrill down her spine. She wanted more of it, a lot more.

She moaned when Ruby wrapped her strong arms around her, lifting her up. Desperate to feel her closer, Hannah locked her legs around her hips, as always in awe of her muscles and strength.

She giggled when Ruby landed them on the pillows, pressing wild kisses on her face as they sank into the heap. She felt giddy, high on life. Every touch from Ruby set her skin on fire and she felt herself get more and more curious about the mating bite.

It was new and mysterious and the thought of doing it with Ruby excited her. Every touch and kiss left a promise of more and as eager she was to get to the bite, she also didn't want the smouldering tension to end. She felt like she could stay in Ruby's arms forever, just the two of them without a care in the world.

Ruby's lips pressed against the side of her face, trailing kisses down her jaw and down her neck. An involuntary moan escaped Hannah's lips as she tipped her head back, sighing when Ruby suckled on the sweet spot under her ear. Now that she had Ruby's hot lips there, she almost regretted choosing her wrist.

"Are you still okay?" Ruby murmured, coming up for air.

"More than okay," she confirmed, sitting up slightly. "I'm ready."

"You sure?"

She presented her marked wrist to her new wife, realising she was trembling with nerves and anticipation. She had a good idea of what to expect but just like most things in life, it had to be experienced first hand. Even so, she steadied her breathing and nodded. "I'm sure."

Ruby pressed a light kiss on her wrist and the mark pulsed in response. Hannah gasped from the sudden jolt of heat shooting through her body and straight to her core. When she heard it would give her pleasure, she hadn't expected it to be like this. Ruby brought her other wrist to her red lips, kissing it with a little bit more intensity. A moan escaped

Hannah, the heat in her lower belly growing from all teasing.

She locked eyes with Ruby, admiring the wild fire flickering in them. Her breath hitched when Ruby's teeth extended into fangs and she brought her wrist up. She held still, the anticipation crackling in the air as Ruby brought her lips to her skin. Pleasure shot through her as the fangs sank into the soft of her wrist, the sudden jolt of pain heightening her senses. Her body tingled as the magic surged through her, embracing her as it coursed through her veins and filled her entire mind and soul.

A moan forced itself from her lips and she relished in the pleasure pulsing through her. The mark glowed under Ruby's lips and stayed searingly hot even when she pulled back.

"Are you okay?" Ruby asked, her gaze locked with Hannah's. "Did that hurt?"

"It felt wonderful," Hannah whispered, pulling Ruby up so she could kiss her. She pressed her lips on hers and unabashedly let her hands roam over the other woman's body, hoping to convey the burning desire growing in her.

She gasped when Ruby's hand deftly snuck under her shirt and she cursed herself for not undressing first, desperate to feel her skin on hers.

With much less consideration for her own shirt

than Ruby's, Hannah yanked it over her head, not caring if she ripped the fabric or where it landed. Goosebumps rippled along her skin, the sudden change in temperature providing an interesting contrast with Ruby's hot skin.

"Someone's eager," Ruby chuckled, her voice hoarse.

Hannah hitched her leg up between Ruby's thighs, grinning when she felt the smouldering heat and heard the other woman gasp. "I'm not the only one," she remarked confidently. It felt good to reciprocate, to know she was just as turned on.

Hannah gasped when the woman on top deliberately shifted her weight, the new pressure pushing her knees apart. She eagerly let her legs fall open further, inviting her in.

"You're gorgeous, you know that?" Ruby breathed, her hands roaming over Hannah's body.

There was desperation in her touch, Hannah noticed, an urgency that echoed her own. She grasped at Ruby, driving her hips up. "I want to feel you inside me."

Ruby lifted herself slightly to snake her hand between their bodies and Hannah's breath hitched in anticipation. The gentle touch didn't satisfy her aching need and she dug her nails into Ruby's arm. "No teasing."

"Are you sure?" Ruby returned, her smirk growing while her touch remained featherlight.

Hannah squirmed, trying to create friction of her own but every movement only added to her desperation without providing the pleasure she craved. Just when she thought she couldn't take it anymore, Ruby's fingers slid inside her and she gasped from the sudden fullness.

"Is that what you wanted?" Ruby breathed in the nape of Hannah's neck.

In response, Hannah released a satisfied moan. She could feel Ruby's body set the rhythm, her hips driving her hand into her. Hannah's breathing sped up with every movement and the mark on her wrist pulsed rhythmically, growing warmer and stronger. It felt like a faint heartbeat, one that matched the woman on top of her.

Hannah gasped when she felt Ruby's teeth grazing her earlobe and she twitched in response.

"You do like it," Ruby grinned, her voice laced with bemusement and a hint of pride.

In retaliation, Hannah dragged her nails down Ruby's back and the other woman sped up the rhythm, clearly encouraged. Satisfaction laced through Hannah from knowing her so well and she placed wild kisses on Ruby's hot skin, encouraging her to keep going.

Hannah's eyes locked with the the other woman, the fire in them bigger and brighter than ever. She laced her arms around Ruby's strong shoulders, her fingers trailing over the silver scars. The pressure and heat in her lower belly built with every thrust and she knew she was getting close.

With one last drive of Ruby's hips, the tight coil in her stomach whipped free and Hannah cried out at the same time as Ruby tensed. Waves of hot pleasure rolled over her and she shuddered and shivered, digging her nails into the other woman's skin in a desperate attempt to get her impossibly closer.

Her wrist burned and the magic of the mating spread through her body, filling every fibre of her being with Ruby's essence. It joined with hers, a comforting presence that spread to the furthest corners of her soul and she knew she'd never be lonely again.

"Mine," Ruby whispered, the fire smouldering in her eyes.

"Yours," Hannah confirmed, leaning in to kiss her wife and mate.

EPILOGUE

R<small>UBY</small>

D<small>UST</small> F<small>LUTTERED</small> through the air as Ruby dropped another cardboard box in the entry hall of Hannah's flat. Well, their flat, considering she was officially moving in.

"How many more?" Hannah asked from behind her, huffing and puffing.

Ruby stepped aside so the other woman could enter, grinning at the dishevelled sight. Hannah's flushed face was practically the same colour as her scales and she had to admit she quite liked the colour on her. It just looked right.

She pulled Hannah in once she'd set her load

down, her hands landing on the other woman's hips. "Come here for a kiss."

"I'm all sweaty," Hannah protested, pulling back slightly.

"I don't mind."

"I do."

"Fair enough." Ruby threw a kiss instead and gave her a little pat on the bum. "Let's get some more boxes."

"Maybe one kiss wouldn't hurt. It's not like you've not seen me all sweaty before," Hannah said.

Ruby grinned as the other woman pulled her back into the house, her lips finding her own. With Hannah's hands roaming over hers, the heat from the moving quickly changed into a different kind. The mark on her hip shot tingles down her body, a warm reminder that they were always connected.

A thud sounded from behind them and Kendra knocked on the wall. "Hey hey, save that for later. Rubes! I'm out here slaving away and you're getting it on with your mate. My poor lonely heart."

Ruby pulled back from Hannah with a last kiss, the two of them giggling at being caught. She flashed a cheeky smile at her short-haired friend, not really bothered. "You could find a mate if you didn't keep kicking women out of bed before breakfast."

"Nah, I'm good on my own." Kendra gestured to

the two of them. "Although I have to admit, you two make it look pretty sweet."

"It is," Hannah said as she took a sip from a stray bottle of water. "I can always give you Jodi's number, it seemed like you two hit it off at our wedding."

"I'll pass on dating your ex, thanks," Kendra replied dryly. "That just feels like asking for drama."

Ruby chortled. "You dated mine for a bit. Remember? Bebe? Actually, she also went out with Aisling and half the other girls in our year."

"So she did. She was fun, I should give her a call sometime." Kendra pondered for a moment and nudged back to the moving van. "Anyway, we should lift the table while we're still in good shape and then you two can go back to... celebrating."

Laughter filled the house and with a shrug, Ruby did as her best friend asked. It took until night fall to unload all her things and after a round of pizza, she said goodbye to Kendra.

"Thank you for helping me move." She pulled her best friend in for a tired hug. "Are you sure you're okay being in the flat by yourself?"

"Of course. Besides, I've been preparing for this moment since I met Hannah. I could tell she was the one for you."

"How?"

"The way you looked at her, spoke about her. I

felt jealous, not because I wanted you for myself or something, but because I realised you found the thing we're all looking for." Kendra kissed Ruby's cheek and patted her arm. "I'll be fine, I promise. I don't need a mate, I'm happy by myself."

"Famous last words," Ruby teased. "You never know, maybe one day, a woman will walk into the bar that'll change your life."

Kendra chortled. "I doubt it, but if it happens you'll be the first to know."

With another hug, they promised to see each other soon, and Ruby returned to the house. Despite having practically lived there for six months already, it still felt a bit different to walk in through the front door. Now it was her house, her home. All her stuff was here and so was Hannah.

She chuckled as she found her mate passed out on the couch. A long day of moving would do that to a human, she thought. For a moment, she watched the sleeping woman, overcome with affection. Being mated was truly something else and none of her friends' descriptions had lived up to the reality of Hannah. And now, she'd get an eternity with her.

Not wanting to disturb her sleeping mate, she turned the music off and tidied away the pizza boxes.

Hannah jolted up from the sound of the bin, looking slightly dazed. "Did I fall asleep?"

"You did. You should go to bed," Ruby said, gently guiding her off the couch.

"Are you coming too?" she inquired, perking up.

"Of course. I can't wait to sleep in *our* bed in *our* bedroom."

"In *our* house," Hannah giggled, taking her hand and pulling her along. "Come on then, Callahan. Oh, maybe you can do that biting thing again."

Ruby laughed all the way to the bedroom, chasing after her mate with her dragon just beneath the surface. She'd never imagined it could be like this but the pulsing mark on her hip and the ring on her finger promised her a lifetime of Hannah.

She had found her treasure.

Signed Paperback & Merchandise:

You can find signed paperbacks, hardcovers, and merchandise based on my series (including stickers, magnets, face masks, and more!) via my website: www.arizonatape.com/shop

My website also has a selection of free stories and books that'll give you a taste of my other works: www.arizonatape.com/free

* marks a finished series

Modern Fantasy

Stories set in a modern setting with elements of magic and slow-burn romances.

- The Griffin Sanctuary
- The Forked Tail

Paranormal Romance

Paranormal romances that will make you swoon with happy endings for the couples.

- Queens Of Olympus
- Crescent Lake Shifters
- The Hybrid Festival
- My Winter Wolf*
- Purple Oasis with Laura Greenwood
- Aliens and Animals with Skye MacKinnon
- Twin Souls Universe* with Laura Greenwood

Urban Fantasy

Continuous adventures in urban settings with a dash of action, danger, or mystery, and slow-burn romances.

- The Afterlife Academy*
- The Samantha Rain Mysteries*
- Amethyst's Wand Shop Mysteries with Laura Greenwood
- The Vampire Detective* with Laura Greenwood

Contemporary Romance

Romances in a contemporary setting with happy endings for the characters.

- Rainbow Central*
- Twisted Princesses*

ABOUT THE AUTHOR

About Arizona Tape

Arizona Tape is a European author who enjoys nothing more than creating new worlds with nuanced characters and twists on mythology from around the world.

Her stories often contain a fantasy element with the focus on inclusivity, diversity, and representation. Whether it's dragon shifters looking for their fated mates or demons hiding in the human world, there's always an element of romance and discovery from a modern angle.

Growing up, she could be found making multiple trips to the library on the same day or sneakily reading under the covers past bedtime. She still writes most of her books at night.

She lives in the UK with her girlfriend and adorable dog, Fudgestick, who is the star of her newsletter. Sign up here for adorable pictures and free books: www.arizonatape.com/subscribe

Follow Arizona Tape

- Website: www.arizonatape.com
- Mailing List: www. arizonatape.com/subscribe
- Facebook Page: http:// facebook.com/arizonatapeauthor
- Reader Group: http://facebook.com/ groups/arizonatape
- Bookbub: http://www.bookbub.com/ authors/arizona-tape
- Twitter: http://twitter.com/arizonatape
- Instagram: http:// instagram.com/arizonatape
- TikTok: http://www.tiktok. com/@arizonatape

Ingram Content Group UK Ltd.
Milton Keynes UK
UKHW040734210723
425555UK00004B/190

9 798223 012047